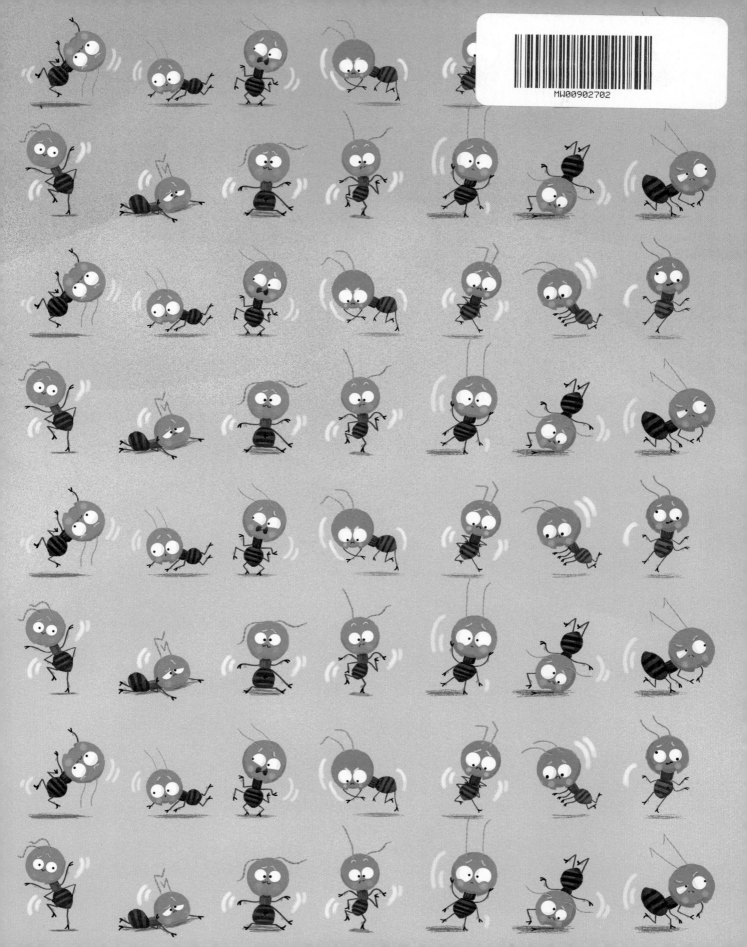

© 2022 Sunbird Books, an imprint of Phoenix International Publications, Inc.
8501 West Higgins Road   59 Gloucester Place   Heimhuder Straße 81
Chicago, Illinois 60631   London W1U 8JJ   20148 Hamburg

www.sunbirdkidsbooks.com

Library of Congress Control Number: 2020945955

ISBN: 978-1-5037-5713-4 Printed in China

The art for this book was created from pencil sketches that were finished up digitally using a tablet and digital pen. Text set in Bryant and Carneval Normal.

THE ANTS WHO COULDN'T DANCE

Written by Susan Rich Brooke
Illustrated by Paul Nicholls

sunbird books

On a bright, sunny day, some ants—a big bunch—
were waiting together to bring home their lunch.
As they listened to music, the ants took a chance,
but try as they might...

...the ants **COULDN'T** dance!

You see, dancing, for ants, is especially tricky.

They have three left feet, which are really sticky.

The ants couldn't **SWING** or **SHIMMY** or **SHRUG**.

They couldn't even dance the **JITTERBUG**.

"The picnic is over!" one ant called to the rest.
It was time to do what ants do best.
They **LIFTED** the food that was left behind
and **MARCHED** away in a long, straight line.

A squirrel shook her tail to say, "How do you do?"
which made the ants wish they had tails to shake, too.
"Will you teach us some moves?" they asked the squirrel.
But the ants couldn't **SHAKE**...

or TWIST...

or TWIRL.

Try as they might, their dance moves felt wrong.
So the ants formed a line and marched along.
They reached a puddle, and without breaking stride,
they **BUILT** a bridge to the other side.

A beaver waved "Hi!" to the ants on their route,
which made the ants wish they had hands to spread out.
"Will you teach us some moves? Nothing too big."
But the ants couldn't **CLAP**...

or **TAP**...

or **JIG**.

The ants tried their best, but it just wasn't good,
so they formed a new line and marched through the wood.
They reached a tree, and without standing still,
they **DUG** in the dirt to make their hill.

A bird flapped "Hello!" to the ants while they bustled,
which made the ants wish they had feathers that rustled.
"Will you teach us some moves? We're willing to try."
But the ants couldn't **DIP**...

"That's it," one ant said. "I can **LIFT**, **BUILD**, and **DIG**.
But I'll never be able to **TWIRL**, **DIP**, or **JIG**.
It's time to give up on my dancing dream."
Then another said, "Hey! What if..."

"...we dance as a
TEAM?"

And just like that, without taking a rest,
the ants all did what ants do best.
They formed a line that stretched out wide
and then **MARCHED** together, side to side.

They **MARCHED** in and out, and up and down,
back and forth, and round and round.
They formed a circle, a star, and a heart,
doing together what they couldn't, apart.

"That'll teach us," one said, "to stop saying 'can't.'
A line dance is just the right dance for an ant!"
"And marching's not all an ant can do.
Let's **LIFT**," said another, "on the count of two!"

The ants used their strength and teamwork skills to **BUILD** a dance pyramid, high as the hills. Soon the forest was filled with claps and chants and whistles and cheers for...

...the ants who **COULD** dance!

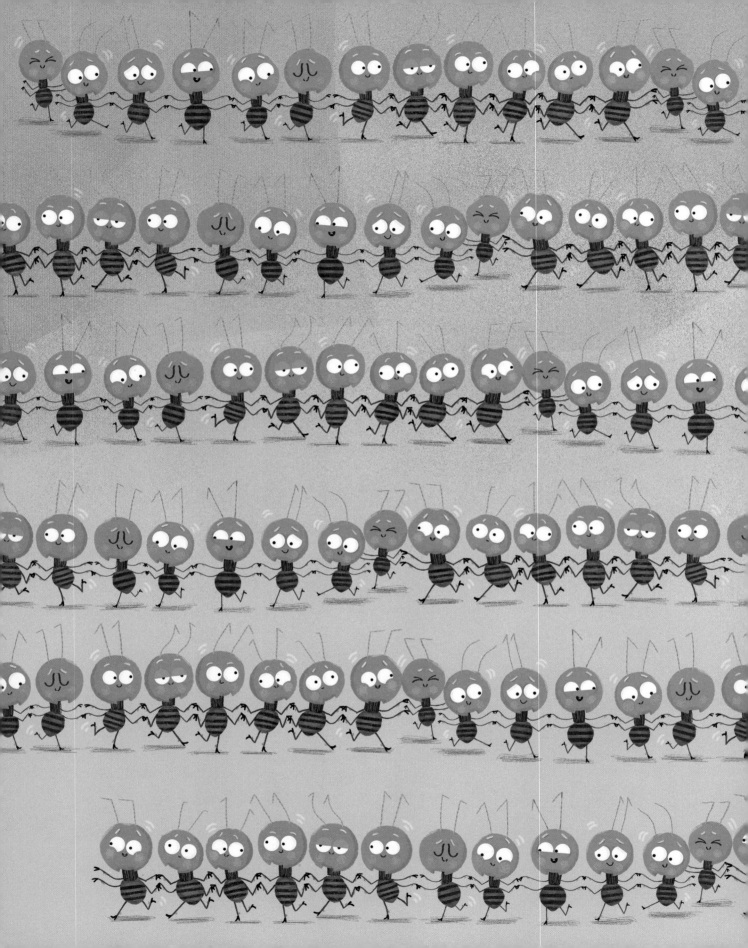